# A Princes
# A Prince
# And A Dragon

## by Joan Harris

## Illustrated by Christi Thomas

**Taylor and Seale Publishing, LLC**
Daytona Beach Shores, Florida

Copyright 2014
ISBN: 978-1-940224-63-3

*Page layout by whiterabbitgraphix.com*

# A Princess, A Prince And A Dragon

## by Joan Harris

Illustrated by Christi Thomas

To Charley, John, James and Paul who taught me just how much joy there is in reading with children.

Through the woods and over the ocean in the far-off Kingdom of Kool
lived the lovely princess Betty Lou Sue.

She liked puppies, wearing beautiful dresses and fancy hats,
and playing the kazoo.

But sometimes she was bored. On one of those boring days, she looked out her window. There she saw the dashing prince Arthur Jim Ray riding on a handsome white horse.

"Yoo-hoo!" the princess called as she waved her scarf out the window.

"Hey ho, lovely princess," the prince replied. "I am off to round up dragons. Want to come for a ride?"

"I'll be right there." She put on her favorite dragon-hunting hat and rushed out to meet the prince.

"Allow me to help you climb on my horse Lightening with me." The prince leaned over and helped her mount. "We're off! By the way, I love your hat. it's perfect for a dragon hunt. It could be very scary. You know how dragons are."

They traveled many miles through forests and small villages, over many fields, through streams and up and down hills.

"Are we nearly there? How much longer? Should we stop for directions? I think we passed that pink castle three times before," Betty Lou Sue complained to the prince.

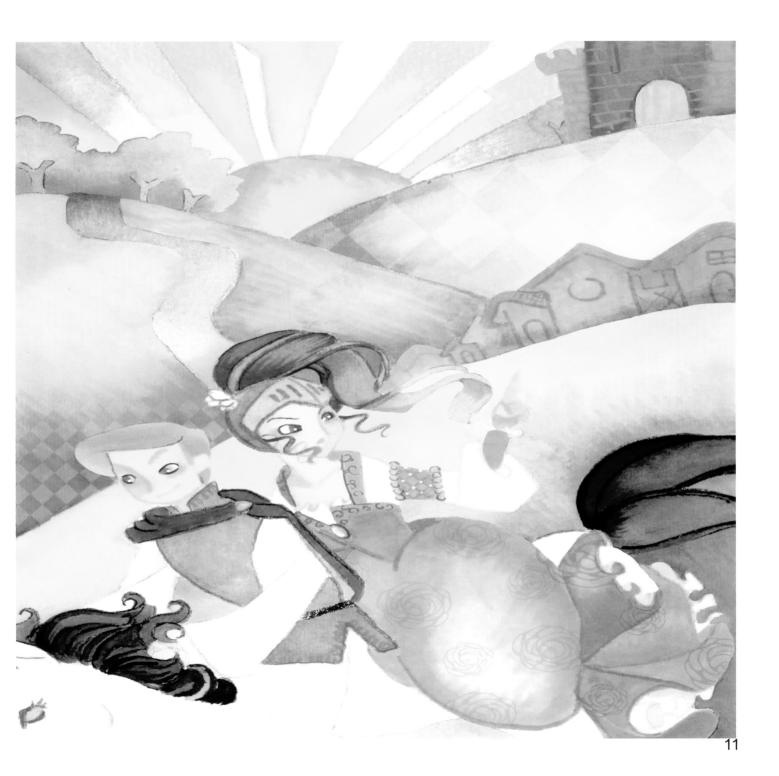

"Never fear! We're getting close to Dragonville very soon now. it's just beyond the next curve, I think."

"They traveled on for several hours, and then the prince shouted,"There! There it is! Dragonville!"

The princess, who had fallen asleep two hours earlier, woke up, rubbed her eyes and read the sign, "Welcome to Dragonville -- Home of the World's Friendliest Green Dragons!"

"Great!" whooped the prince excitedly. "Now I just need to find the caves where the dragons live."

They found a dragon cave. On the door they read a note. Home of Billy Joe Bob, Dragon Extraordinaire."

No one answered, so the prince shouted again. "Dragon, beware! I am the prince, and princes always get their dragons!"

Still no answer. The prince put his ear to the door and listened carefully. He heard some yawning and shuffling about. Just then the door opened and a very large dragon asked, "Why are you disturbing my nap?"

"Excuse me. I didn't know dragons took naps. I am Prince Arthur Jim Ray. I am here to capture you and take you back to my castle."

The dragon dropped to his knees while big tears rolled from his eyes. "No! No! Please! Please! Please! I am really a fine dragon, a very friendly fellow. Can we talk?"

"My mind is made up. there is a cage waiting for you. I will show all my friends how brave I am by capturing you and bringing you home with me."

Betty Sue Lou walked over to Billy Joe Bob. She began to dry his tears with her scarf. "He really is a cute green dragon. Let's listen to what he has to say."

Billy Joe Bob wagged his very large tail and leaned over to give the princess a kiss.

"Look, he's just like a great big puppy. I do so love puppies."

"Oh. I can be better than the best puppy you have ever seen."

Then Billy Joe Bob snorted and great flames of fire came from his nostrils. "What do you think of that?" he asked.

"It's a very hot day, and I don't really need any fire," the prince replied.

"Oh, but watch this." Billy Joe Bob leaned back into his cave and found what he needed. Foofth! More flames! This time he handed the princess and prince two perfectly melted s'mores he had made with the fire. "What dog can do that?"

"Hmmmm, that is quite a feat," the prince admitted.

"That's not all. I'm great with barbeques. Shis-ka-bobs are my specialty. And I sing and I dance and I play the kazoo."

"You play the kazoo?!" the princess exclaimed.

"Quite well, people tell me. I've been to Kazoo College, and I always lead the dragon kazoo parade."

The princess ran over to Billy Joe Bob. She motioned for him to lean over, hugged him and said, "Billy Joe Bob, you would make a wonderful pet. Why don't you come home with me?  I will take great care of you. I will teach you to fetch, shake hands, roll over and play dead. You could be the perfect dragon puppy."

"That's nice, but I need more good reasons if I decide to move to your kingdom."

"Well," said the prince, "The Kingdom of Kool is a very fine place. We have a music festival and a concert hall where you could teach and play the kazoo. There are beautful parks where you could barbeque. The people would love you."

"My palace has many extra rooms. You could have your own room with a balcony. I would see to it that you had the finest green dragon food brought to you, and I would be your special friend," said Betty Lou Sue.

hmmm...

31

Billy Joe Bob looked the prince in the eye and asked, "You won't try to make me live in a cage?"

"Well, I guess any dragon who can roast a marshmallow is extraordinary. Come with us and be our special friend. There will be no cage for you."

Tha dragon thought for a moment and then held out his hand. "That sounds like a good deal. Let's shake on it. I already know how to shake hands. Let me go in and pack and I'll follow you to your kingdom."

Billy Joe Bob packed all his marshmallows, his graham crackers and chocolate bars and his shish-ka-bob skewers.

Then together they began their trip to the Kingdom of Kool. Along the

way, BillyJoe Bob taught the prince and princess the words to some of his

favorite dragon songs which they sang while he played the kazoo.

They reached the Kingdom of Kool at sundown where they all

lived happily ever after.

# ACTIVITIES:

A. Discussion

1.  Why did the prince ask the princess to go with him on this adventure?

2.  Do you think she liked the idea he had for the day?

3.  What gives you the impression that she does or does not want to go out?

4.  Do you think his idea of a good time sounds like fun?

5.  Is the dragon what you imagined him to be?  Why or why not?

6.  Is the princess what you expected her to be?

7.  What do you think of the prince and the princess?

8.  Would you like to learn more about them?

9.  Can you think about more adventures they might have?

B. Art

1.    Draw a picture of your idea of a prince.

2.    Draw a picture of what you think the princess should look like.

3.    Draw a picture of a dragon.

4.    Draw a picture of what you think the dragon's home should look like.

5.    Draw a picture of a castle.

C. Writing

1.    Could you think of another ending to the story?

2.    Could you tell or write a princess story of your own?

# About The Author

**Joan Harris**

Joan Harris, a Licensed Marriage and Family Therapist, lives in New Smyrna Beach, Florida with her husband, Charles. They are the parents of four grown sons and are now enjoying thirteen grandchildren, which helps explain Joan's interest in writing for children.

Joan is a member of Florida Writers Association and the Society of Children's Book Writers and Illustrators. She is an award winner in the 2013 Royal Palm Literary Society and an award winner in the 2014 Royal Palm Literary awards:
First Place  RPLA  Educational/ Informational Category *"Beating Bullies"*
Third Place RPLA Flash Fiction Category *"Reflections"*
Finalist RPLA Flash Fiction *"Searching for Grandpa"*

# About The Illustrator

## Christi Thomas

Christi Thomas was born in 1987 in Savannah, Georgia. She received formal training at the Savannah College of Art Design, where she pursued and attained a degree in Illustration. Since graduating, Christi has found her niche in children's book illustration, where she enjoys crafting whimsical and fantasy pieces using a variety of media. Christi has volunteered extensively and has seen first hand how creativity can enhance and brighten the life of both children and adults alike, and now strives to bring that creativity to as many people as possible.

This is her second book for Taylor and Seale Publishing. She is now working on a sequel to this book entitled, *The Royal Dragon*.

This book may be purchased through:

Amazon.com and Amazon Kindle
BarnesAndNoble.com
Books-A-Million
TaylorAndSealePublishing.com


Educational packets for teachers,
as well as bulk orders, may be
purchased  through:

Taylor and Seale Publishing, LLC.
2 Oceans West Blvd., Unit 406
Daytona Beach Shores, Florida 32118

Phone: 1-888-866-8248

CPSIA information can be obtained at www.ICGtesting.com
Printed in the USA
LVIW01n1046210415
435131LV00007B/9